MW01699263

WARN DOMINGUEZ

BLOOD RAIN

TRANSLATED AND AFTERWARD
BY
KIRK LAYTON

ISBN 978-0-9783776-0-1

Published by Kirk Layton

Email: khlayton@shaw.ca

A special thank you for the help with this project to Maria Jacketti, Diana Patterson, and Robyn Starkey.

PARA MIS MUCHACHAS

I

To the western edge of the city of Calgary, cornered on two sides by rows of houses and on the other two sides by the TsuuT'ina native nation is a stretch of undeveloped land.[1] That is to say undeveloped as much as any land can be in a time of prosperity. Years ago the city had set the land aside for a future four lane road and major interchange.[2] Until it was needed, city official built a pathway system and a park that became popular. Families arrive each weekend and park their SUVs and BMWs for a chance to commune with nature. They bicycle down the asphalt pathways with the yellow dividing line clearly marked as to not challenge an oncoming cycler or in-line skater. Sometimes, when the blood that falls most afternoons seems chilly, they congregate around one of the several covered picnic spots to warm hotdogs and 7-11 burritos.

It was one of those Saturdays when the park seemed extra full of condo dwellers who had woken from their five day dream with a desire to feel grass on

---

[1] Calgary, Alberta, Canada. The undeveloped area is known as The Weaselhead, a part of North Glenmore Park.

[2] A reference to the Calgary transportation "Go Plan" prepared in the 1970s.

their feet.[1] They gathered in a rather large area of green where they slipped off their shoes and socks. The grass was sticky with the musk of deer that disappear during the day but at night chose this same spot to copulate.[2]

The company presidents and oil firm engineers[3] put their faces to the grass, breathing deeply and enjoyed the erections the musk caused. Their wives and lovers waited at home, with lights turned low and alcohol free wines on the dresser, to be taken repeatedly as the reward for feeding the dreamers during the week.

Rose stood overlooking the scene with the Rockies penetrating the sky to the western horizon. Behind her a bank manager took a mouthful of grass and washed it down with a large Chi tea. Directly in front of Rose, the earth gave way in a jagged cut sliced by ice during a February freeze.[4] You could see the levels of time in the exposed sediments. Layers of volcanic ash over a seabed containing the remains of

---

[1] The dreamers are a probable reference to Gabriel Garcia Marquez's novella *Innocent Erendira*.

[2] The Weaselhead is home to animals that are seldom seen until dusk.

[3] Calgary is a major business centre with many oil company offices.

[4] Some park paths are next to a cliff that erodes.

extinct marine creatures were now high above sea level.[1]

At the bottom of the cliff was the water. To the north was a meandering stream that had long ago twisted back on itself, eating at the banks that confined it, until it created new paths and forgot about the older ones. The water started high on the mountains to the west where blood rain fell as pink snow until melted by a sun that rested on its shoulders.[2]

Just below Rose the water joined other waters that had been directed to this spot to form the drinking supply for the city.[3] They didn't belong together in this way. At times they had fought with the loser being shoved over a rocky bank where it found its way into basements and gutters. The waters had learned to cooperate to some degree. Rose could see the motion as one water chased another around the reservoir. They were not too serious at this end of the reservoir. It was when the new waters had finally pushed them to the eastern side did they realize that they were to be used. That is when they really would

---

[1] Geology students are taken to this location to see the layers. Calgary is 1048 metres (3440 feet) above sea level. This is also an early reference to layers of time.

[2] Rocky Mountains

[3] Glenmore Reservoir

fight for a chance to avoid the treatment plant that added fluoride and chlorine and rotted their souls.[1]

Rose stood by the cliff for a moment longer thinking about her decision. The two men sitting at the bench watched her while trying to appear they weren't. One jotted notes on a page while another kept dabbing his nose. Rose removed her clothes and placed them in a neat pile as to not interfere with the joggers who kept to their allotted path regardless of how close the path came to the edge.

There had been a case only the spring before when a section of the path had been sliced by the ice. Before someone thought to fix it, several joggers and cyclists had simply gone over the edge and floated away until dumped unceremoniously onto a farmer's field.

Rose stood motionless than raised her arms to form a cross and leaned forward.[2] She fell a couple feet before the west wind caught her; sustained her; held her in its grasp and let her float forward over the waters below.

"That was you again," said The One Who Writes.

---

[1] Plebiscites were held allowing for fluoride to be added to the city drinking water.

[2] Christian allegory

"I know," said The One Who Always Watches, "but it's not that bad. Looks like fun, don't you think?"

"Do you think it will work this time?" asked The One Who Writes.

"Just write it down. And try to keep it in the same language this time."

"Not my fault. They keep changing it. Hey, you're the one who gave it to them." [1]

"Shhh," said The One Who always Watches, "Here we go."

Rose had floated over the middle of the reservoir. Circled slowly and begun to descend. The waters saw her. They formed a ripple to show her a good spot. There was a slight bulge around it as the older waters joined the new to get a good spot to watch.

At the end there wasn't that much to see. The wind, growing weary, had, when Rose was a couple feet high, let her fall. There was nothing but the sound of a slight plop. The water made sure she was cushioned.

"No big splash? Well that's disappointing," said The One Who Writes.

---

[1] Theological reference to the origin of languages.

The One Who always Watches didn't answer. His eyes were closed. His brow was wrinkled as he began to concentrate. The blood coming was from his nose.

*****

Proceeds from the Art and Soul Conference, Baylor University, Waco, Texas, June 17 2000
Speaker: Johannes Burg, D.D.
Trinity College, University of Toronto.[1]

"I would like to start by thanking the chairperson of our convention, Dr. Anne Baker and the chair of this session, Professor Elliott Pearson. I'm sure all in attendance will join me in thanking them for the excellent work they have done in organizing a conference of this degree.

There are many here who object to my use of the colloquialism, The Book.[2] While most people outside of academia do refer to it this manner, I do acknowledge that it is not a complete or independent collection. Indeed, it does not take an academic to recognize the gaps that take place in the text.[3]

What I would like to discuss, in the few minutes I have, is the latest feelings concerning the what we refer to as The Sand Papers and if it should be considered part of The Book of The Transformation. First, let's not even bother talking about the Death Lines that were mistakenly added in 1616. There has been enough research to indicate that those poems

---

[1] An annual conference. This location may have been chosen for Waco's historical association to the Branch Davidian sect.

[2] Theological reference without specifying which religion.

[3] In literary theory, "gaps" must be filled by the reader.

were indeed written by Chaucer and not, as was claimed for so long, a translation from a fragment of text that was destroyed later in a house fire. [1] I'll pause for a moment while we all suffer a collective groan over the generations of academics that dutifully studied and published commentaries on this lie for so long.

In 1996, while charting the Athabasca tar sands in northern Alberta, three employees of Shell Oil discovered several pages of parchment in a stone box. [2] We have all seen the cell-phone photos that appeared on the internet within minutes and remember the riots that happened when followers, or Bookers, as they call themselves, felt it signified the transformation. So many climbed towers or went to roofs of tall buildings to lean into the wind and forgot the rule about height and depth of water...ah well.

Last year saw the release of the scientific study of the stone material itself. While the original thought was that we would hear it was yet another staged event by Bookers, it became evident through the science that was employed that the material was authentic. To further add to the proof was an

---

[1] Some scholars believe Shakespeare may have written sections of the King James Bible

[2] The tar sands contain more oil then Middle Eastern countries but the oil is difficult to extract from sand. The box alludes to containers for religious documents that have been found.

indication that the same tools were used to create it as was used for other boxes. Remember, not the same type of tools, but the actual same tools.

That brings us to a discussion today about the text itself. The delay in interpretation was in that we were attempting to use the Rosetta stones that had been present at other finds. They, of course, did not work in this instance. In the chance that there had been something yet to be discovered around the site I travelled to Athabasca and examined the location personally. There was nothing else to be discovered. Out of frustration I decided to take a vacation and decided to see a part of the world that I was unfamiliar with. I travelled north.

As you can imagine there is not much to see in Northern Canada when you have the eyes of someone from further south. Like many, I was hoping to see how the deer disappear which takes on a different appearance when the angle of the sun in the north plays with the optics of the illusion.

What I found was something unexpected. I had the opportunity to share a meal with a family of Dene, the traditional people of the north. [1] While I was discussing the text that I had attempted to commit to memory, one of the elderly women in the family began to sing it. It was at that moment that we realised

---

[1] There are many groups that make up the Dene. This group sounds like Inuit of the far north.

that what we had was not a dead language but a very early form of a traditional language in an obscure dialect. The problem was that the Dene did not have a written form of this language and there was no clear way to translate. We gathered all the elderly people together and when they recognized a part of the text read to them we were able to match what they sang to what was written. Through that we have created a Rosetta stone and have, so far, translated about one third of the text.

The most significant lines include the following:

Water turns upon itself
as the time follows.
The watcher goes back to
find the blood to re-enter
that which will be
and once was.

As we have seen in the past, the references to water, the watcher, and blood are present. There is also a mention of time and possibility that it is not linear but possibly circular or reoccurring.[1] No, I am not going down that line of discussion as it is best left to the experts in that area. I know many of you don't like to

[1] There are a variety of ideas about time within the first nation peoples of Canada and the United States.

even hear about those possibilities, but, given that lines that have been translated, we may have to reconsider our beliefs."

*****

Ivy stood beside the farm house her husband's father had built shortly after they were married five years before. The valley soil was rich with nutrients for the grains to supply the city only a short drive away.

Ivy wiped her hands on her apron as she ignored the faces on the valley cliff to the east of her. She was used to the men that stood there, threatening her. She had learned to ignore them, even when they pointed their rifles and shouted profanities.

She walked down to the stream that ran through the valley. For the past couple of years she had been watching this section with fascination. The stream had begun to chew away at the back and was ready to loop back on its self forming a cut bank and then an oxbow.[1]

She had read the signs in The Book. This was a sign. This was the proof that the water could help her.

When she had married she had been ready to assume the expectation of a good Canadian wife. She had opened herself to her husband and waited for the

---

[1] Cut banks and oxbows are common in western Canada.

sickness or the moods that her mother had warned her about. When she had waited long enough she had looked for the answers.

Ivy remembered the year that followed. She had asked questions. Then nice men, in pairs, with nametags on their suits had arrived at her door. Young couples with their children had followed. Each had a book or document or story that acted to prove they had the answer. The all claimed The Book was either wrong, or incomplete, or the translation was a mistake.

So, Ivy read The Book herself. Half way through she had read of the water; she had walked to the stream by the farm house; she had a realization. "When the water chases the water and the circle is formed it is time." She remembered the lines by heart. "When the water chases the water the blood rain fills the vessel that is empty." This is the line that had her heart beating. "When the circle is formed the vessel dipped in the water will be filled with the blood." It was there, right before her. The bank of the stream giving way to form a circle and with it the chance she would have.

A couple weeks after her reading the lines that changed her life Ivy had learned of the plans from the city close to the farm. They were going to damn the water downstream. They claimed that the city was growing and they needed the drinking water. Between the stream and extra water taken from the Bow River they would have a drinking water reservoir that would last for generations.[1] Ivy knew that would mean she would be the last of her line.

She had fought the plans. She had gone to city council meetings. She had lost.

Now Ivy stood beside the stream. The water was around her ankles as she removed her blouse and skirt.

The One Who Always Watches stood on the cliff beside the angry men. He was thinking hard.

"Is there time?" asked The One Who Writes.

"Just write it down."

"But is there time?"

Ivy removed her undergarments as the water reached her waist. The blood rain began to fall, but only lightly.

"There isn't time, is there?" asked The One Who Writes.

The blood rain began to fall heavier and the west wind got stronger. Ivy raised her arms and formed a cross as the water rose to her throat.

---

[1] When the Glenmore reservoir was formed, farm land and several farm buildings were flooded.

It was then it happened. The wind. It had always blown down from the mountains to warm the land but this time it also had another quality.

The angry men watched has it pulled Ivy. Played with her. Caressed her. Lifted her from the water and took her to another place where she would never see their faces again.

"She wasn't ready?" asked The One Who Writes.

"There wasn't time," said The One Who Always Watches.

*****

They stood facing west, as was the rule, with their arms perpendicular imitating the flights taken by the chosen or the fortunate ones.[1] Some bore the scars of old wounds they had suffered when they attempted to soar, but had, instead, plummeted from the cliffs to the ground below. Some were men who had travelled around the world to each of the locations where various documents had been found.[2] Others were women who had dreamed of being chosen. Those women that gave up that dream stood next to their

---

[1] A play on facing east to pray as this appears to be a western based theology.

[2] Resembles a modern form of a pilgrimage.

husband and children. Older women that had never surrendered the dream stood with each other hiding their anger at being childless. Young women who believed it could be them stood together in the centre of the group. They were protected and, all too often, isolated lest their identity be discovered and their virginity taken by unbelievers. They remained in that position as the invocation was given.

"Blessed be The Watcher. Blessed be The Book. Let us who follow the currents of the water and chart the path of the wind have the strength to overcome. Let us not disappear into the sunlight but soar above the unbeliever to become the vessel for The Watcher. Blessed be the Watcher. Blessed be The Book."

*****

They had only been at the camp for a few days when the stories had begun to arrive. The messengers ran, as they always had, from the big waters in the east to the base of the jagged cliffs.[1] Through their trip they met many peoples and they had to learn to speak the languages of each nation. Here, the TsuuT'ina had long had the duty of looking after the land for the Father Who Watches. The runner had learned their

---

[1] First nations messengers were famous for their running ability.

language long ago and recognized her. Each year she was older. He spoke to her in the language of her people and smiled remembering her name was taken from the white flowers that grew on the prairie.

"Daisy," said the Running Man, "Have you heard?" [1]

"I have heard what the elders are talking about," said Daisy, her simple coverings barely hiding her breasts from the glances of the messenger. "Is it true they kill the deer for fun?"

Daisy had long before climbed the cliffs they camped beside and found the deer. They had come to her and let her touch them as if she were one of their own.

"They kill without need." He reached out, taking a breast in one hand.

"I will say a prayer to The Father Who Watches." Daisy pulled on one part of her covering and it fell to the ground. "I will ask that they cannot see the deer when the light rises in the east."

She lay on the soft grass next to the stream that supplied the camp with life. She watched the deer and she had watched her people. She was unsure how The Running Man would like to mate with her. Some liked it as the deer and placed their women on their hands and knees while others placed women on their backs.

---

[1] Daisy is not a first nation name.

Daisy stayed on her back as the messenger entered her. Her virgin blood spotted the grass and then, as a light rain fell, became part of the stream where it was chased by the other waters.

The One Who Always Watches saw the waters chasing the blood and knew that this was to be the spot.

"But she is not the one?" said The One Who Writes.

"No," said The One Who Always Watches, "she has given her blood to show where it will happen."

"If this is where, then when?"

"We must wait until the water is ready. It must have a say in this."

*****

Proceeds from the Learned Societies Congress, The University of Western Ontario, May 28, 2005
Speaker: Meyer Stopp PhD.
California State University, Los Angeles.[1]

"Thank you for your warm reception. During the past couple days we have experienced rain in Ontario, but not, of course, the rain known as blood rain. I want to remind us all of the basic history of the rain and then discuss the implications of this latest occurrence in Canada.

Some say it was first recorded in Peru during a major rainstorm. There had been several mud slides and it was believed that during the slides that some earth had been picked up by the wind. The muddy earth was carried high and mixed with the moisture in the cloud until it returned to earth in the form of a reddish coloured rain. The stories of that first occurrence are oral, of course, and formed the backdrop to several legends.

There was the belief that this was the blood of warring gods and that the victor would soon appear to claim the land that had been fought over. There was also the belief that was falling was the tears of a god saddened by the faults of the people. Both of these legends lead to theological debates that resulted in the

---

[1] Meyer and Stopp were two men who analyzed red rain and found it contained chloride of cobalt.

death and oppression of many in the society. There was also the legend that this was the earth attempting to revive itself by showering itself with blood. This resulted in the practices regarding fertility rites related to sustaining the land.

The rain that fell in China created serious problems that lasted for generations. In the early 15th century the two primary dynasties had fought a battle that had lasted for ten years. When the Tung clan appeared to have won the reddish rain fell over much of the country. It was believed that the rain was blessing on the clan and indicated God supported this family. The brutal nature of this family cannot be overstated, and anybody that did not support them disappeared. Evidence indicates that as much as one third of the population was slaughtered before the family collapsed due to internal struggles and assassinations. The difference between the effects of the rain becomes significant when you see the scars present today on Chinese society compared to the earth friendly culture of Peru.

The rain has been reported in several areas of the globe besides Peru and China, such as Naples, Italy in 1818 and then 1890, in Messignadi, Calabria.[1] It appears that the rain must fall over a longer period for

---

[1] The rain in Naples was thought to contain volcanic dust. The rain in Messignadi was said to contain blood from birds killed in high winds although no bird parts fell.

people to be affected by it in some psychological or philosophical manner. This is why the blood rain in Canada is of special interest.

There had been sporadic instances over the past few years in Chibougamau, Quebec, and Come-By-Chance in Newfoundland.[1] Five years ago the rain began to fall almost every afternoon in or, at least, near the city of Calgary in Alberta. A team of researchers is there and are, as we meet, carefully charting and testing the rains. They have been met with threats of violence from The Bookers, while the local authorities and residents do not even acknowledge that they exist."

*****

Rose swam down; the fish that call the water home on either side of her. At the bottom of the reservoir she saw the cabin and beside it a tepee made of the skins of many animals.

She could still see the original stream that had flowed for generations. The fish guided her to an older oxbow that formed a circle.

Rose lay on her back on the muddy bottom of the reservoir as grass grew around her.

---

[1] Actual Canadian cities.

Sitting on the bench beside the walking path an elderly looking gentleman sat alone looking at the water below. He took out a journal and began writing. The blood rain that was falling was heavier than anyone had remembered.

-W

*****

Excerpts from a tract titled The Beginning distributed by The Church of the Book of Transformations, 1962.

1. From before the time that was measured there were the waters in the forever.
2. The waters were both the givers and the takers and over the time they began to argue.
3. The waters that were givers began to join together
4. The waters that were the takers began to join together.
5. When they had split they found a balance.
6. In that balance they found the ability to create and destroy.
7. If the balance is destroyed then all must end.
8. During the time that was not measured they realized that there was a purpose.
9. They created.
10. The water that creates formed The One Who Always Watches.
11. The waters that destroy formed The One Who Writes.
12. The waters teamed together and formed those who walk.
13. In time, the ones who walk separated into those that create and those that destroy.
14. Those that create began to produce blood.

15. When they could produce the blood they could create others who walk.
16. When the waters experienced the joining of the blood both the waters that creates and the waters that destroy knew a new greatness was soon to come.
17. They sent The One Who Always Watches to find one who walks to aid the transformation.
18. They sent The One Who Writes to record the events.

*****

II

Later that day Rose sat in her kitchen drinking herbal tea while the visions she had while swimming collided with each other. Fragments that appeared at first to be real became dreams, and dreams interfered with reality as she took another sip. She reached for the honey to sweeten the tea as the feeling of warmth and comfort again swept over her. It was just a momentary feeling but it was exactly the same that she had felt while beneath the waters of the reservoir. She was confused. How could this water that she bathed in, that she watered flowers with, that she had even made her tea with, have such another sensation? She had The Book on the shelf, wedged between the *Corpus Hermeticum* and the Kafka novella she had read in university.[1] Most had The Book. There was a time when it had been given to every school child.[2] Now, though, you were more likely to get it handed to you at the mall by some smiling non-descript woman.

On a sudden impulse she ran through the house making sure every door was opened. She sat

---

[1] *The Corpus Hermeticum* was originally thought to be pre-Christian in origin, but it is now known to be an early Christian document from Hellenic Egypt. Kafka was a writer of magical realism.

[2] *The New Testament* used to be given to all Canadian students.

down somewhat perplexed as her husband had long commented about her insistent need to close those same doors. A fixation was what he had referred to when she had risen from love making to close the bedroom door.

"Honey, there's nobody else here."

"Just wait."

"Ah...come on...who cares?"

Truth was, she cared. She always had worried about doors. As a child she had lain awake until her parents were snoring and then she had quickly and quietly gone through the house making sure each and every door was closed. She was never sure if she was keeping something out or keeping something in. So, what did this opening of the doors now mean? She finished her tea and put the cup in the dishwasher, not even realising that she propped the dishwasher's door open a couple inches.

At 6:15 Charlie walked through the back door. Not 6:10, not 6:20, but precisely 6:15. He took the 5:30 train from the 7th street station to Westbrook Mall. At the mall he transferred to the number 18 Lakeview bus. He exited the bus at the corner of 32nd street and Lakeview Drive and walked the two blocks to his house. He did not talk to anybody during the trip home. He did really see anyone else and they didn't appear to see him. He worked downtown. A simple statement, but one that for the residents of Calgary summed up everything. A few years ago someone had realized that it had happened. There was no report that it was happening, as, obviously that had been occurring for many years. It had simply become a way of normality and even those that did not work downtown saw no problems with it. Charlie was a sleeper. Perhaps not the correct medical term, but the word that most used to describe it. It was a fugue that affected the conscience of those that worked in the downtown core. Medical authorities suggested pollution, but those comments were ignored. The Bookers claimed it was another sign of a transformation, but they, as always, were laughed at. The philosophers pointed out that the work being done by oil company executives and advertising writers and the ever present middle managers was such a waste of time that the global consciousness of those involved could not cope.[1] In response, they turned off part of the brain and appeared to go through the work day sleeping and moving with their eyes open. In this way he had travelled home, oblivious to the middle aged man wearing an ill fitting suit with pens in his shirt pocket who was watching him through bifocals and taking notes.[2]

---

[1] A probable Kafkaesque political reference

[2] John Fowles placed himself as an observer in *The French Lieutenant's Woman* and this description resembles the author of *Blood Rain.*

There is a routine that happens in life that only gets broken by short burst of the unexpected. For Rose, her brief flight and the swim that followed was just one of those breaks. Her life appeared to most to be a recurring series of days that started precisely at 6:00am when the clock radio broke through dreams with the voices of the CBC newscasters. It ended at 11:00pm when, having washed the sweat of the world from her body, Rose folded back the covers and climbed into bed carefully as not to wake her husband. Perhaps to those who do not take the time to notice, all things were part of the routine, but there is one who does notice. Normally there would be two, but since the swim there was only one left taking notes. He noticed the opened doors at first. He then saw Rose trying to keep cupboard doors open as well. When Charlie insisted on closing them she took a hammer and a screwdriver and removed the doors altogether. Charlie had started to ask but the look on her face indicated that she had no idea what he was asking about. Charlie soon forgot about it as well.

On weekends Rose would jog to the park and stretch before taking her place with the other joggers on the path. She would jog along the asphalt pathway that formed an artery that crisscrossed the city.[1] As the pathway bent to the reservoir, Rose would stop and look west over the water and towards the

[1] Calgary has an extensive path system.

mountains. It was here she felt an inner peace and an inner turmoil at the same time. At night she had fragmented thoughts of a home under the water where a woman had once stood. Sometimes there was another younger woman lying beside the water.

"No, that's not it," she murmured to herself on one such occasion. "Not just any woman...me. That's where I stood."

Rose had a momentary desire to strip and fall into the water to look again but changed her mind. She let the west wind kiss her cheek before she turned back to the path and began to jog once again.

*****

The following story was found in the Calgary Herald newspaper three months later.

Reports indicate that in the three months since the fall of heavy 'blood rain' no other rain of that type has fallen.

There has also been a controversy with the Canadian Water Network/canadien de l'eau that was in the city to study the phenomena.[1]

They reportedly had just taken samples when the rain stopped.

The samples taken show no signs of any foreign substance. The water is said to be pure.

As rainwater itself is never pure there are claims of errors or sabotage to the study.

The Bookers are once again claiming that this is a foreshadowing of their claims.

Residents of the area of Lakeview are increasingly concerned about the large number of believers who are congregated at the reservoir to practice their rituals.

There have been reports of violence towards them.

City police point out that the area The Bookers use is not on city property.

It is reservation land and only the reservation police have jurisdiction of the property.

The phenomena known as 'blood rain' has appeared in several locations in history and reports indicate it often stops without any reason.

*****

[1] An agency of the Canadian government that identifies issues with Canadian water.

There are many who collect information on their families. There are others who do their best to track the genealogy of the family back as far as possible. Rose was one of the latter types. At least, she tried to be a person like that. The trouble was the gaps that kept appearing in the lineage. She knew the major reason for this. She just didn't like to admit it to herself, or to Charlie. There was a slight problem that kept appearing with the women in her family. It didn't seem to make that much sense because if you looked at the lineage as a bloodline, it was not direct. There were adoptions. There were illegitimate children. At the very least, women married into the line, so any physical reasons should not have existed. There were numerous reasons why it would not make sense that so many women in Rose's lineage had difficulty conceiving.

Rose kept the paperwork and the photos she had collected in the top drawer of the bureau. She made a pot of herbal tea and put her collection on the kitchen table so she could spread them out. There was something here, something she had been on verge of seeing. She was sure of that.

When the doorbell chimed she moved to the door and greeted the young man and woman who were there.

"The time of the transformation is at hand, so if you would only give us a moment we can explain the various reasons why you should believe as we do and act now...."

Rose did not even attempt to interrupt them. They were so use to the negative reactions that they didn't even pause for breath. When one ran out of air the other would pick up the narrative in mid-sentence.

"...and by the time the transformation occurs all believers must bow into the wind to join the..."

Rose was not listing to them. Her attention was drawn beyond where they stood to sidewalk in front of the property. She had seen the man before, of that she was sure. It was the when and where that she had trouble placing. He was nondescript in many ways. He looked elderly but moved like a younger man. Rather short and getting plump with glasses that forever seemed to slip off his nose.

"Writing, that was it...that's what he's always doing," she thought to herself, "I wonder what that's about?"

She didn't bother to listen to the couple at the door. She had failed to even remember that they were there as she walked away, leaving the door open. She had begun to do that at regular intervals, much to Charlie's chagrin. The Bookers stood there for a few minutes, not knowing if they should enter or wait for her return. Their rule about going into houses was very clear. Ever since one of the believers had thought he had permission to go into a home and had been shot at, they had decided to make sure the invitation was clear. They looked at each other but decided that an offer to enter had not been made so they simply turned and went onto the next house. They didn't even notice the gentleman writing on his notepad.

Rose returned to the table and began to spread out the information she had collected. She found herself staring at a photo for some time. Its sepia tone was faded to an almost indistinct brown. But there was something about the face as if she had seen it before. She rifled through the collection until she found a pencil drawing that had been done by a rather artistic member of the RCMP. She placed the young native face beside the photo. The resemblance was not evident at first, but the longer she looked she began to realize there were similarities. She checked the names of the women: Ivy and Daisy. She walked around for a few minutes staring at the photos and stopped in front of the fireplace. She looked from the photos in her hand to her marriage picture on the mantle. When Charlie arrived on schedule she was still standing there with a look that alternated between disbelief and understanding.

*****

Excerpts from a sermon titled The One given by L. Russell Smith, President of The Church of The Book of Transformations, 1964.[1]

"One of the concerns that followers have is the notion of the chosen one. Unlike other fundamentalist sects that observe the power found with The Book, we believe that the chosen one is not arbitrary. We know that our beloved, albeit misguided brothers and sisters who became the Reformed Bookers, think that the one is a regular woman. They misinterpret The Book as stating that the one woman will be chosen when the waters are ready. What we know is the use of the word "the" should be considered in its grammatical form. It is a definite article. It means, not any woman, but the specific one. As such it must be recognized that if there is only one then that same one must always be the one The Book speaks of in several places. In the third chapter of Samira, found in the Netherlands, it refers to the attempt made with the one during a storm that destroyed an entire fishing fleet.

We must pay attention to the wording in this section:

---

[1] L. Ron Hubbard founded The Church of Scientology, Charles Taze Russell founded the Jehovah Witnesses, and Joseph Smith founded The Church of Jesus Christ of Latter Day Saints.

1. She lay with the maker of seed.
2. She lay as the time before.
3. The many times before.
4. The Watcher was ready.
5. The water was ready.
6. The wind was not.
7. All must agree before the time is right.
8. Let all wait for her return as before.

There is only the single woman who is chosen to act as a vessel for the return before the transformation occurs. There is every indication that she does not know that she has been chosen, but that she returns to the world until it is successful. It becomes an imperative that we view all women as being the potential one. As we agree with this we must take steps to protect and teach them wisely. This means we must introduce some ideas and concepts regarding the treatment of women within the church.

The following rules have been approved by the council and go into church law immediately: [1]

1. All women are considered vessels of The Transformation.

[1] The rules are a combination of rules concerning women from a variety of societies and religious practices.

2. All women must wear white until they are joined with a man. (bridal gown)
3. All women are to cover their heads, arms, and legs. (muslim)
4. All women must receive daily education in how to behave.
5. Women may not be in public without the company of a man.
6. Women may not smoke, drink alcohol, or eat red meat.
7. Women who disobey may be punished.

We know that there will be women and men who do not agree with the new laws from the council. Those who protest will be removed our records. They will be placed on the list that must never be talked to for any reason.[1] Let them suffer when the one is found and let them ask for forgiveness when the transformation occurs.

Blessed be The Watcher. Blessed be The Book."

*****

[1] A style of excommunication and banishment used in some religions.

Rose sat waiting. She had flipped through the old editions of Time and Newsweek without really reading anything. The doctor had made some efforts towards modern technology as he had recently installed a television in the waiting room. Most of the time it was soap operas that most women who came here were interested in. At some point it had been flipped to the CBC news station. It was the flash on the screen that had caught her attention first. Then the smiling, always blonde, news anchor said something about a live breaking event in Chile appeared on the screen. The sound was low but Rose could read the text crawl on the bottom of the screen: "...leader of obscure Booker group...originally from Germany, moved to farm by Santiago...raping young women...farm raided..." [1]

Rose suddenly became angry as they were showing the event live when the sect leader was taken from the farm house towards a waiting vehicle. The emotion grew within her, radiated from her, directed towards the clean cut smiling man on the television. She could see his face clearly. She could see his white teeth, his blues eyes, and his perversion. Rose did not hear it. It was a single word that emerged from her lips, "vengeance."

---

[1] Paul Schaefer moved from Germany to Chile in the 1960s with a religious sect that practised child abuse. Under his orders, no babies were born to sect members for 25 years.

The faces of the Chilean officers began to change and started to look confused. The wind had hit them hard and, yet, appeared to come from all directions. It pushed them away from their captive as the cameramen did their best to keep the event in focus. The wind isolated him, wrapped around him, and, at first, seemed to caress him. He stood smiling thinking he had found salvation when the first blow hit. The wind began to batter him as he was standing. It kept him in one place has it repeatedly slammed into him. The officers were helpless as the wind pushed them back whenever they tried to intervene. They stopped trying and watched with amazement. The wind picked up pebbles and then larger stones, driving them into flesh and then bones.[1] At the same time the wind held him in the shape of a man until it began to take small pieces away. The last part to disappear was the face with the look of horror still on it. - She controlled the wind

The scene had returned to the anchor woman in the Toronto studio. She looked puzzled for a moment as she looked off camera. Rose read her lips, "Where were we? Alright, let's go to Colleen for a curling update." [2] Rose was already forgetting what she

---

[1] Symbolic of a ritualistic stoning of offenders in both Biblical and modern eras.

[2] A probable reference to championship curler and CBC commentator Colleen Jones.

had seen. There had been a problem, but the problem had been removed. Besides, the bonspiel was more interesting.

When Rose returned home she acknowledged the man that was watching her, standing as he often did in front of the house. The first time she realized he was always there she had felt a moment of panic. It had changed into a calmness that was only enhanced by his presence. She had nodded to him a few weeks ago and watched laughing as he had run away. Now, he just nodded back and returned to his writing.

She walked through the entry way into her house. You couldn't call it a doorway anymore. [1] There simply wasn't a door there, or anywhere in the house for that matter. She felt the wind in the house touch her cheek and then leave to be replaced by wind that was cooler and fresher. On the living room carpet Rose had arranged photos, letters and diaries that had gone back several generations. She had become keeper of the family history and knew there was that one thing she was seeing that was never acknowledged by any member of the family. Men had no problems; in fact, they seemed only too able to propagate. It was the women who had what one diary entry had referred to as "the difficulty." Not all the women, but

---

[1] Christ can be seen as the door between the separation of God and man. The removal of the door may indicate that either the separation or Christ does not exist.

there appeared to be a line that, when placed beside each other took on a lineage of its own. Charlie had looked at it and laughed. "Not how that works at all," was all he had said. Yet Rose could see it buried there between all the dates and places. It was a line that led directly to her. But if she was right then something else was not. She had to lower herself slowly to the floor, feeling the wind hold onto her elbows so she would not stumble.

*****

The citizens of Calgary have always followed the weather. They know the importance of snow and rain in relation to the crops. Even those that had never been to a farm knew that a heavy snow pack in the Rockies to the west and the spring rains always meant for a green springtime in the many parks. During the cold winters days each person would glance west several times a day. They were looking for the line of blue over the Rockies that signified the Chinook winds. [1] The larger area of blue they saw the happier they would be, knowing that a break to the winter doldrums was on its way. That was why the morning commuters were smiling. They knew something was coming, so did Rose.

---

[1] A Chinook is a warm dry wind that flows down from the mountains in southwest Alberta.

Rose had called family ahead of time. She had not wanted a hospital or their doctors to be around. This was a special time, not just for her, but for the women in the family. They had begun arriving that morning. Distant aunts and cousins each prepared to help in any way they were asked. They had entered the master bedroom and, finding it suitable, had begun to clean. The bed was stripped of its blankets to be replaced with fresh white linen. The room was emptied of all other furniture and then the process of washing started. Never had the hardwood gleamed as brightly and the walls looked as if a new coat of paint had been applied. One elderly aunt had sat Rose into a chair had washed and combed her hair. There was, for a few moments, stuffiness to the room as if it had become crowded. The aunt had not looked up, but sensing the crowd had merely pointed to the open area leading to the outside and said, "Some of you leave...now." Only the older wiser winds had stayed and they made sure that the impatient ones stayed out for the rest of the afternoon.

The sun was half way behind the Rockies when the Chinook winds hit the house.[1] For generations that were countless it had been their job to absorb the excess water and snow and chase away the cold. They were looking forward to this extra duty.

[1] Although thought of as a winter event, Chinooks happen year long.

They were the final line of protection towards any that would object. There were those that had long followed the signs that had seen them, followed them, and wanted to be there. Part of the group was made of devoted believers but others wanted to stop it. It did not matter. The Chinook had been given its name long ago and the modern translation of the ancient word was snow eater. In the old dialect of the Cree, however, it was the decoration that women wore on their wedding night.[1] It was a talisman meant to protect the bride from harm while acting to symbolize fertility. The talisman itself had fallen out of use during the invasion of the white hordes, but the Chinook had never forgotten the role given to it long before time.

The Chinook surrounded the house, absorbing the snow that had fallen on it and creating a barrier. Those that had started to arrive who were not welcome found the force of the wind held them back. They could see the house. They could see the missing doors leading inside but could not penetrate this invisible shield. Groups of men in suits and holding books dropped to their knees. Women, some in white, tried to lean westward but found the wind refused to support them any longer and let them topple over to the ground. Charlie had arrived home on schedule and the others watched as he simply walked through the

[1] There is no evidence of this being true.

wind and into the house. The elderly aunt had given him a can of soda and directed him to the den where he could watch a hockey game. His presence was not required at that time.

Rose lay back on the clean sheet and closed her eyes. Even then the images took shape. She saw layers as if looking at multiple images at the same time. In the days of film cameras this would have been more than a double exposure and there were more layers then she could count. If Rose concentrated, she could focus on an image, but only for a moment. She saw scenes of an ancient land where warmth was difficult to create and language was something new. Right away that was replaced by a school of laughing youngsters dressed in white and just as quickly a vast prairie appeared accompanied by the beating of many drums. Instead of confusing Rose, these images comforted her. This was her past and her future, her beginning and her end.[1]

Rose raised her arms and the winds that had waited outside entered from all the openings she had created in the house. They found her; lifted her; held her. Droplets of water taken from the river were brought to caress and cool her brow. The women she had invited stood back from the bed and sang a lullaby.

*****

---

[1] An illusion to alpha and omega

III

Excerpt from Views of Time and The Church of the Transformation, delivered by Professor Gary Sparling of the University of Mount Royal, at the Science in Religion Conference, University of Pittsburgh, July 14, 2087. [1]

"Thank you for the warm welcome I have been receiving all week. It was difficult for me to come out of retirement to speak to you. Mind you, it's difficult to do much of anything at my age.

I guess it's due to my age that there has been a resurgence of interest in myself and my dear beloved mother. At the time of my birth there was a large amount of speculation and there were the believers that dedicated their life to following me. I think I've outlasted all of them and yet nothing has happened in the world that can indicate any sort of true transformation. Granted the weather has changed. The polar bears are gone. The permafrost of the north is marshland. The Canadian boreal forest has pretty much been wiped out by the mountain pine beetle and the forest fires that followed. My home in Calgary has seen a great deal of flooding and you here in Winnipeg

---

[1] George Sparling is a mathematician who suggests that space-time has six dimensions.

have experienced even more.[1] With these changes the winds that meant so much have changed and no longer support the fliers of the past. The optical illusions that protected the deer are no longer effective. Even the glorious blood rain, as it was called, has stopped. But you know all that. You want me to comment on my research on time. Yes, time, my life's work. You want me to relate it to the old Book of Transformations. Let's get started.

My research indicates that time is not linear, nor is it circular. There is a beginning and an end. I want you to imagine travelling down one of those major freeways that we used to use in the old oil days. Think for a moment of changing lanes. In that instant you have changed the timeframe you are in. You are still progressing but it is possible that the lane of time beside you is already part of what you consider history. Do you want to change it? You can and you can't. Any changes you attempt to make have already been made as they have already become part of what you consider history.

That group that were referred to as Bookers understood a small part of this. However, they were under the misunderstanding that when The One Who Watches returned it would open a mystical gate into a realm of understanding. That was their mistake.

---

[1] Winnipeg has been flooded several times while in 2005 downtown Calgary suffered severe flooding.

If you think of time as lanes in the road then you have to multiply the analogy many fold. There are not a handful of lanes but countless numbers of them. To make matters worse, they are not side by side in any logical order.

Now that you have that mental picture, try thinking of a being that is in the wrong lane. They have to find where they belong by crossing many lanes until they can find their home. Now, if you are still following, what if the being in question was tired of what appeared to be a pointless exercise of frustration and, instead, wanted to settle in a time frame? Not any specific one, but any one that would let it remain before being forced to, again, change time lanes.

That is what the Bookers did not understand. It was never about the transformation of humanity, but of the being in question. Only by taking a form not familiar to it, the human form, could it stop the journey across time.

When you look at the documents that formed the Book of the Transformation, you need to place them beside each other and not chronologically as found or as written. Some of the latest ones were written first as that was the time change these beings were in. There was more than one. They did leave small markers that I have found in the mathematics concerning time. What I had recently discovered in my studies is that in some of the markers there is evidence of countless numbers, but in most there is only evidence of two, and in a handful there is only evidence of one.

The Bookers had believed that The Watcher was responsible for good in the world and would lead us to glory. Some believed in a second being that recorded the details into what became the actual book. I am not concerned with the silliness of beliefs that have died out over the last fifty years. I am more concerned with the mathematical properties of time.

If these beings could cross between the time lanes then there is a question that we may be able to as well. I would like to inform the university that I am making a cash donation to the mathematics department for a new wing. I will be donating all my research with the hope the next generation of scholars can break the puzzle and begin to travel."

*****

He stood in the bedroom shortly afterwards. She saw him and smiled. The small being in her arms did not see him, and never would. She would forget about him over time. He would not forget about her. She had been the first and the child in her arms would be the last. There were not anymore that wanted to end their journey in this way. He knew he could join them if he really thought about it, but that was never something that interested him. He would simply write down what he saw and try to convey to these creatures what they use to be before they settled down.

He stood at the side of a cliff and lifted his arms perpendicular to his sides before falling. He fell not down but across time.

*****

Excerpts from

The Book of The Transformation

Published by The Church of the Transformation (reformed)

2027

THE BOOK OF BEGINNINGS

1 These are the books of the One Who Writes; the keeper of the records from the time before the time that is now. [1]

2 Let all those who read know the truth that comes from those that know as they were the ones that were before who we are now.

3 In the beginning there were the waters and they were as one.[2]

4 The waters waited for the passing of the endless void that was both the start and the end of all things.

5 From the depth they saw the woman who signified the start of time look down from the emptiness that surrounded them.

6 The woman who was the one leaned towards the beauty of the waters until she lost balance and fell towards the endless waters. [3]

7 As she fell, her form changed from one that had no form to one that did. [4]

---

[1] Attributes all the books of the religious document to a single author.

[2] Suggests that nature existed before people and that nature is capable of thought.

[3] In some first nation beliefs, First Woman loses her balance and falls to the earth.

[4] Suggests a spiritual existence prior to a physical one.

8 The waters were ready and cushioned her fall; supporting her in their grasp.
9 It was then that they disagreed as to what the action should be and if they should keep her forever in their arms or to create another place for her.
10 The waters separated into great voids to show how they felt and in doing so exposed what they rested on.[1]
11 It was this that the woman who was first found she could stand on without the help of the waters.
12 Above her was The One Who Always Watches and he knew she needed more than the land for her to survive.
13 He concentrated until plants and other creatures began to take shape on both the land and the waters.
14 The harder he worked on what was needed the more blood came from his nose and fell on the land and waters.
15 The woman who was first took this as the sign that The Watcher was taking care of her.
16 As the woman took charge of that which was around her she felt the passing of time which was a new experience.

---

[1] Creation of oceans and of land.

17 She realized that she was the only one like her and begged The Watcher for others that she might spend her time with.[1]
18 The Watcher gave directions and she went to the waters allowing them to surround her, covering her with their love and admiration.
19 High above one who had asked stood at the verge of the nothingness that was all that was known.
20 He raised his arms from his sides and fell towards that which was below.
21 The winds that had watched were given direction by The Watcher and touched him gently, guiding him towards the woman who was first until he entered her.
22 This was the first to undergo the transformation with the woman who was first.
23 The One Who Watches stated that all those that wanted be on the world must undergo a transformation.
24 He said that all must undergo the transformation in the same way with the same woman.
25 He removed the knowledge of who she was from the woman so she would not know the burden that had been placed on her.

---

[1] Compare to Adam's desire for companionship.

26 For many revolutions of the sun those that had transformed enjoyed all that The Watcher supplied for them.

27 There were some of the waters and some of the winds that wanted their space returned to them and objected to those that trespassed on what was theirs.

28 They worked together to create a being of their own who was made of the wisps of moisture that was angry and held together by the breath of the wind that was angry.

29 This being of anger and frustration could move without being seen to whomever they wanted to upset.

30 They had passed between many and placed questions into their minds about why they were still subjects of The Watcher, and why they could not enjoy their own labours.

31 At last they entered the mind of a woman who had recently undergone the transformation and made her question why only the woman who was first could act as the vessel for those who wanted to transform.

32 She asked a man just as the mist confused him and he agreed to aid her in acting as a vessel for the transformation.

33 They lay together as the mist had instructed them and found as they did a feeling that had not been experienced in their time on the world or in their time before the transformation.

34 As they lay together the sky grew red with the blood of The Watcher whose anger had never been experienced.

35 Those who had undergone the transformation gained the awareness of all of the senses that they were unaware of before.

36 They experienced pain and joy and friendship and hate.

37 The Watcher gave them all that they had asked for except for the one thing that they truly wanted; they could not aid in the transformation.

38 Those who were born to them were beings of their own creation and not beings who had undergone a transformation.

39 The woman who was first was always loyal to The Watcher and had ignored the mists that tried to overcome her.

40 The Watcher declared that the woman who was first would be the one who always aided with the transformation but knew this was difficult in this new world order that was created.

41 He allowed her to return through time with no memory of the past and to, when she was able, act as a vessel for others that wanted to undergo the transformation.

42 He removed any knowledge of who she was from her to protect her from those that did not understand the truth.

43 She was never and will never be alone as she will be under the view of The Watcher at all times.
44 The One Who Watches was not pleased with the world.
45 The mists had taken the thoughts of many who had transformed and many who were born of the world and turned them towards evil things.
46 The Watcher sent The One Who Writes to record the events and leave messages for those on the world.
47 As The One Who Writes fell to the world he found the mists had broken time apart and scattered it so that the pieces of time did not appear in order.
48 He took the story of what had happened prior to the transformation and left it where he thought it would be secure.
49 He took tools and formed a box of stone so that the writing would be protected until it is found.
50 He then wrote what he saw around him and left that as a message to those in the world.
51 The Watcher wanted those beings who transformed to become the pure beings they once were.
52 The Watcher wanted those beings born on the world to become as the transformed beings once were.
53 He gave directions that were written down and placed within the stone boxes.
54 He knew they would be found out of order.

55 He knew those on the world would have to piece the guide together.
56 As he thought about the best way to help his beings the blood flowed from his nose.
57 The blood fell as rain on the world.
58 It became a sign that The Watcher was there and was trying to help.
59 Both those who transformed and those who were born of the world saw the rain and wondered at its significance.
60 Those who transformed had a collective memory that there was a time before and felt the purity that had once been theirs.
61 They strove to reclaim that purity.
62 Those who had been born on the world became jealous as they too felt purity but knew it to be beyond their reach.
63 They formed groups and fought about the best way to achieve a transformation into purity.
64 The documents left by The One Who Writes were found.
65 They were found in the wrong order causing misunderstandings about the method to be used for transformation.
66 They waited for the blood rain to fall and give direction from The Watcher.
67 Blessed be the woman who was first.
68 Blessed be The One Who Watches.

THE BOOK OF THE CLEANSING

1 There was in the fractures of time a concern for The One Who Watches.

2 He saw that the mists had prevailed in their goal and that the evil that they desired was coming.

3 His anger turned into blood rain that covered the lands.

4 He called on the waters that understood and disagreed with what the mists had done.

5 The waters that supported The Watcher gathered to think about how they could help.

6 At first they thought to flood the world but they found that was not fair to those who desired to know the truth of the transformation.

7 They thought to remove large sections of the world and leave other parts untouched.

8 They agreed that in the spring when their power was the greatest they would find parts of the world where the evil was the greatest and work to overpower it.

9 They practiced on small parts of the world using the waters that transect the world.

10 They flowed over the banks that contained them surrounding the beings that were there to give a message about what would happen if the message was not heeded.

11 The beings created dams and levees to control the waters and ignored the warnings.

12 The waters called on the great waters that separated parts of the world.
13 The great waters called on the winds that loved The One Who Watches.
14 Together they came on the land to show the power that those that transformed had ignored.
15 The mists were no match for the great waters and winds and they left to find others whose minds they could cloud.
16 The great waters, with the help of the winds, came on the earth.
17 They were shocked to find beings were still there as if their progress had not been seen.
18 They found those who could not leave and were not helped by those who could.
19 They tried not to harm those but such was their power that many of those who could not leave were swept away.
20 For those The Watcher felt pain.
21 There were those who ignored the warnings and cared not for anything but their belongings and they were swept away.
22 For those The Watcher felt nothing.
23 There were those beings who understood the messages in the writings that had been found.
24 They realized that a transformation had taken place.
25 They supported the mists and worked to obscure the truth from other beings.

26 They believed that they were chosen to return to the time that was before.

27 The great waters asked the winds to find those that kept the truth hidden.

28 The great waters enjoyed finding them and covering them with the power of the waters until the beings were swept away for all times.

29 In this The Watcher felt satisfaction.

30 Let those who know the truth and keep it to themselves know that they will be found and disappear from the world for all time.

31 Blessed be the woman who was first.

32 Blessed be the One Who Watches.

THE BOOK OF MYRTLE

1 In the year of the quake that marked the inception of the reign of King Mordicia, The Watcher caused the blood rain to fall in mighty storms.

2 This was taken as the sign that the woman who was first was present in the kingdom and that the world was ready for the transformation to occur.

3 King Mordicia sent representatives to the four corners of the kingdom to return with all virgins of child bearing age.

4 Hearing that women were to be used by the king for his own purpose, fathers who did not support the king gave their daughters to male neighbours to have their virginity taken.

5 Mordicia decreed that any father who committed such an act would be stoned by the true believers on the last day of the month.

6 Mordicia decreed that any man who deflowered a woman who may be the woman who was first would be castrated on the last day of the month.

7 The messengers returned to the castle with two hundred and fifty four women who were inspected by the elders who interpreted the signs of purity.

8 Those who were found not to be virgins were sent home; those who were found to have a blemish

that rendered them unfit as a vessel were kept as concubines.

9 The total that was left was fifty and six who were placed into gowns of pure white.

10 They were given first to the elders for instruction as to how to behave, how to dress and how to speak.

11 There was one who refused to obey and she was called Myrtle.

12 Myrtle was fifteen years of age and was the daughter of a peasant and a concubine who had worked for the castle until she was found too old by those that frequented the kingdom.

13 When King Mordicia entered the training grounds all women fell prostrate before him with the exception of Myrtle who stood tall with her arms folded.

14 King Mordicia said, "How dare you stand before me. I command you to show me respect."

15 Myrtle remained standing and replied, "Why should I, the woman who was first, lower myself before nothing but a king; I command you to lower yourself before me."

16 King Mordicia was impressed with her and gave her special dispensation to stand in his presence as her behaviour may be one of the signs that she was the woman who was first.

17 The elders were not happy as she was not one whom they believed was the woman who was first.

18 They wanted a woman who was the daughter of a great land owner as he had paid them handsomely to choose his daughter.
19 They informed King Mordicia that there was a series of tests that could be used to check her worthiness and King Mordicia declared that she would undergo those tests in his presence where he could observe.
20 The elders said the first test was that the woman who was first could stand in the blood rain without a single strand of hair on her head becoming wet.
21 Myrtle was locked within a tiny room that contained only a cot and a basin and was fed through a slot in the door that opened onto a great courtyard that the king could see from his window.
22 Four days later the blood rain came again and the elders smiled at each other knowing that in the pouring rain Myrtle could not keep her hair dry.
23 The king stood before his window and raised his hands to signify that the door to her room be opened.
24 The elders were so secure in their plan that they had asked all in the kingdom to watch as Myrtle failed the first task.
25 All watched as Myrtle emerged from the room and walked slowly and boldly through the blood rain to the centre of the courtyard.

26 The rain fell heavily yet not a strand of hair on Myrtle's head was seen to be wet.

27 The elders rushed to the room and emerged with the hair that she had carefully removed from her head the night before.

28 Their cries of cheating could be heard even above the cheers and laughs of all those who were watching.

29 King Mordicia raised his arms again to signify that the test was complete and that Myrtle had passed.

30 The elders examined the texts and declared that the woman who was first had the power to create life in great numbers.

31 Myrtle remained in her room for four days until King Mordicia stood at the window and raised his arms to signify the door should be opened.

32 Myrtle waked to the centre of the great square as all watched to see how she was to create life in great numbers.

33 Myrtle addressed the king: "My great King Mordicia, before I begin there are many who, fearing for their daughters committed acts that your elders said should be punished by death or castration and I stand here to speak for them."

34 "Certainly you, the father to all in the Kingdom understand the bond between the father and child and the desire to protect them."

35 "I ask for you as the king to show mercy on them and remove the sentence that has been placed on them."

36 The king thought for some time before answering, "Let it be decreed that those who were to be punished have been forgiven and are to return home."

37 "Then," Myrtle stated, "I am finished."

38 The elders clapped their hands with joy, thinking they had watched Myrtle fail.

39 She turned to them and said, "In the law of this land a man who has been sentenced to death is considered dead even before the sentence is carried out."

40 "Those men have had the sentence removed and are now alive and I have fulfilled your prophecy by creating multiple lives."

41 The elders looked towards the King who smiled and raised his arms again to signify that Myrtle had passed the test.

42 The elders were angry that Myrtle had once again found a way of passing the test and decided to use a test that she could not pass and would result in her death.

43 They informed the king that the woman who was first must be able to step off the tallest part of the castle and float to the ground.

44 The king was unsure of this test and demanded that they write down the test and read it to the crowd

so there could be no dispute if she should fail or if she should pass.

45 Four days passed until the door to the room was opened and Myrtle walked to the centre of the square.

46 An elder stood next to her and read the text to a crowd larger than had ever been seen in the kingdom: "For this test to pass we all must clearly see Myrtle float from the top of the highest tower to the ground below."

47 Myrtle began to climb to the tallest part of the tower through a long winding stairwell.

48 As the stairwell passed the room the king was in a door opened and he faced her.

49 Without a word he embraced her, much to her surprise.

50 She gained the top of the tower and stood at the edge trying to think what she should do at this point.

51 It was then she felt inside her pocket and pulling it out realized what it meant.

52 She took the single flower the king had placed there and released it, watching it float to the ground as the crowd cheered.

53 The elders again protested but the king reminded them of the words of the test and that they had all watched the myrtle flower float to the ground without harm.

54 The king declared the tests to be over and that Myrtle was the woman who was first and was also suitable to be his bride and the queen to all.
55 Blessed be the woman who was first.
56 Blessed be The One Who Watches.

AFTERWARD

MAGICAL REALISM IN *BLOOD RAIN*

Although it has been said that magical realism is nothing more than science fiction written in Spanish, the reality is that it contains specific elements. Some of the components of magical realism are placed together with the motif of science fiction in the novella *Blood Rain*. Warn Dominguez combines these genres with a commentary on religion to challenge the reader.

In a parallel to the stories of many of the first nation peoples the role of women is emphasised. Within the creation stories, First Woman falls from the sky to be aided by the creatures of the sea who take soil from the sea's floor to build her a place to live. Dominguez does have the theme of a woman falling from the sky but gives the water and wind that are present cognitive abilities. This is in direct contrast to the Christian story of Adam being the first human and Eve being considered secondary. In *Blood Rain* the role of women is at first strengthened. This role is challenged as it is the males who control the religious nature of society. The being referred to as The One Who Watches is a God-like figure who is also male. However, within native spiritual beliefs there is a symbiotic relationship between male and female figures that must be maintained.

The repeated use of flower names to represent women can be seen as misogynistic were it not for the strength the women also possess. The women are able to gather an understanding about how to control nature and men for their benefit. The flower symbolism is present more for its association with reproduction themes and should not be seen as derogatory.

The theme of there being a group that came from the spirit world and another that were only born of humankind is a direct reference to traditional Calvinistic beliefs. Those that underwent a transformation have the ability to return to purity much as Calvin's chosen. The others, regardless of their actions, cannot transform and are in the Calvin category of damned. However, unlike Christian thought there is no devil figure that comes from the spirit world. The evil force is a made from natural elements that cloud rational thought. This takes native beliefs that spirits inhabit the natural world and extends them into the genre of magical realism. Water, often the symbol of life, combines with wind to form evil.

The development of a religious book becomes a focal point to the novella. Dominguez takes elements from several different beliefs in creating a religion that is based on a record that is misinterpreted. He also suggests that the records that are considered a religious document are not complete and more parts to it may be found. This is a direct parallel to several current religious groups; however, the documents are found around the world as opposed to any specific geographic area.

With magical realism, time is an element that authors can change to suit their needs. Dominguez presents a novella that parallels the description of time he gives towards the conclusion. The narrative is broken into small sections that appear, at first, to be out of sequence.

While magical realism does not require an author to explain magical elements, there is some explanation within the novella. The reader learns that deer disappear due to an optical illusion and that people fly if the water is deep and the wind strong enough. Unlike science fiction no other explanations are needed in these areas. Readers must suspend their disbelief and take these events at face value.

KIRK LAYTON

ABOUT THE AUTHOR

Warn Dominguez teaches at the Albuquerque Universidad de Espanola. I first met him at a conference in Albuquerque and then had the pleasure of working with him later when he came to Calgary to teach Spanish for a couple years. Warn believes that magical realism is a form best suited to the Spanish language and, while in Calgary, was inspired to write *Blood Rain*. He later asked if I would translate but refused to assist in what became footnotes for the text as he believes that clarity is not needed in magical realism. He is currently working on a collection of poetry.

KHL

ABOUT THE EDITOR

Kirk Layton grew up listening to the stories told by a Canadian father and British mother. Following an abbreviated stint in high school he enjoyed a career in media. He later returned to university to study literature. He now teaches literature and composition classes while writing short stories, novellas, and poetry.

By WARN DOMINGUEZ

INDIRECTA DEL SIGLO

NADA ES VERDADERO

ESTO NO ES UNA PISTA, NI ES ÉL

By KIRK LAYTON

CROSSINGS, A NOVELLA OF THE CANADIAN WEST

CHARLES GORDON / RALPH CONNOR: FROM BLACK ROCK TO REGINA TRENCH